Billy, Brush Your Teeth!

By Pamela Malcolm

Aryla Publishing

For my nephew Kèvon.

Billy Series
Billy Go To Bed
Billy Get Ready For School
Billy Brush Your Teeth
Billy Eat Your Veg
Billy Tidy Up Your Toys
Billy's Halloween
Billy's Fireworks Night
Billy's Christmas
Billy's Day Out In London
Billy's Easter Egg Hunt
Billy Goes Ice Skating
Billy Goes Swimming
Billy Series Bundle Books 1-5
Billy Goes to Spain

Ruby Series
Ruby Won't Use Her Potty
Ruby's New Shoes
Ruby's Christmas
Ruby No More Binky (Dummy)

Emergency Services Series
Fiona Fire Engine
Percy Police Car

"It's time for Billy to have his bath. Billy loves playing with his toys in the bath.

"Don't splash too much," Mum says, washing him with a sponge.

"Sorry, Mum," Billy says, laughing. He wishes his alien friends, Floo, Choo and Sloo, from the planet Zobloo were here.

Mum gets Billy out of the bath and dries him with a towel. She dresses him in his pyjamas.

"Billy, brush your teeth" she says. "I'll make your bed."

Billy doesn't want to brush his teeth. Brushing teeth is boring.

"Ok, Mum," he says.

Billy looks out the window at the stars. Somewhere out there are his alien friends. If only he had something to see them.

Billy sits on the toilet and has an idea.

He grabs the next sheet of toilet paper hanging from the wall. He pulls at it until all the toilet paper lies in a pile on the floor. He then removes the cardboard tube.

Billy has invented a planet-finder. Standing by the window, Billy looks through his planet-finder at the night sky. If he can find Planet Zobloo, he might be able to see his alien friends.

Billy looks as hard as he can. All he can see are the moon and stars. No Planet Zobloo.

"Billy," Mum calls from the bedroom. "It's story time."

Billy hurries into his bedroom. Mum tucks him into bed and reads him a story.

Afterwards, she kisses him and asks, "Billy, did you brush your teeth?"

Yes, Mum," says Billy sleepily. Soon he is asleep

Mum goes into the bathroom. "Billy!" she mutters. Billy's toothbrush is still dry. There is a pile of toilet paper lying on the floor.

The next night, Mum dries Billy after his bath. "Billy, brush your teeth," she says, squeezing toothpaste on his toothbrush. "No messing around tonight."

"Yes, Mum," says Billy.

Mum leaves to make his bed. Billy hopes his alien friends will visit tonight.

Billy sits on the toilet and starts to dream. His bath toy ship lies on the edge of the bath. He picks it up. If only instead of a sea ship it was a spaceship.

Billy waves the ship around. The air is still a bit misty from his bath. Space mist! he dreams. Full of tiny planets and stars.

His spaceship dives and soars in the space mist, heading for Planet Zobloo and his alien friends.

Billy!" Mum calls. "It's story time."

Billy hurries into his bedroom

After his story, Mum kisses him and asks, "Billy, did you brush your teeth?"

Billy nods and is soon asleep.

Mum goes into the bathroom. "Billy!" she mutters. Billy's toothbrush still has toothpaste on it and his bath toy is lying on the toilet seat.

The next night, Mum dries Billy after his bath. "Billy, brush your teeth," she says. She wets his toothbrush and squeezes toothpaste on it. "If you don't brush your teeth they will fall out."

Billy nods, red-faced. "I will, Mum," he says. "Sorry."

Mum goes to make his bed.

The aliens still haven't visited Billy.

"The bathroom is steamy from Billy's bath. Billy sits on the toilet and has an idea. He will write a message to his alien friends.

Using his finger he wrote, 'ALEINS VISIT BILLY, on the steam in the mirror above the sink.

Billy!" Mum calls. "It's story time."

Billy hurries into his bedroom.

After his story, Mum kisses him and asks, "Billy, did you brush your teeth?"

Billy yawns.

"Billy?"

But Billy is already fast asleep.

"He dreams he is back on Zobloo and his three alien friends, Floo, Choo and Sloo are with him, smiling. Billy loves being on Zobloo.

His alien friends are having a picnic. All the food and drink is spread out on a bright orange tablecloth on blue grass. Zobloo's pink sun shines warmly down with a big toothy smile.

"Try a chewy banana roll," says Choo, handing Billy a plate with two purple pastries.

"They're yummy."

"And have a fizzy sausage-ade," says Floo.

He hands Billy a glass filled with a dark green bubbly drink. It tastes delicious, just like crispy sausages.

Billy bites on a banana roll. All he can feel are his bare gums. Shocked, Billy feels his mouth. His teeth are gone.

"What's the matter?" asks Sloo.

"My teeth are gone," Billy cries.

Choo munches on his banana roll. "Billy, didn't you brush your teeth…?"

"First thing in the morning…" says Floo.

"… And last thing at night? adds Sloo.

"Choo waves the magic toothbrush at Billy and makes three circles in the air. Then he bonks Billy on the head with it.

Billy feels his mouth. All his teeth are back. What a relief!

"The magic toothbrush only works once," Choo warns.

"You won't get another chance," adds Floo.

"So, don't forget," says Sloo. "Twice a day…"

"Billy, brush your teeth!" the three aliens say together, laughing.

Billy wakes up. He sits up in bed and checks his mouth. His teeth are still there.

Later, Mum goes into Billy's bedroom to wake him.

"Billy, brush your teeth," she says.

Billy is not in bed.

"Billy?" She hears Billy in the bathroom.

Billy is at the door. He is brushing his teeth so hard, his mouth is covered with toothpaste.

"Billy!" Mum says. "I've never seen such good brushing."

THE END

Thank you for reading……..

Please remember to leave a review if you enjoyed my book it would be nice to hear what you and your children thought of this book ☺

Thank you for your time.

Pamela

If you enjoyed this book please also check out these books in the Billy, Ruby and Emergency Services Series below.......

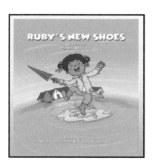

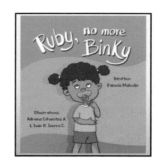

Check out **Billy's Vlogs Monthly** on **YouTube** to find out what he has been up to.

Please visit **www.arylapublishing.com** for more books by **Pamela Malcolm** and other great Authors. Sign up to be informed of upcoming free book promotions and a chance to win prizes in our monthly prize draw.

You can also follow us on **Facebook Instagram & Twitter**

Thank you for your support!

Other children series published by Aryla Publishing

Author Casey L Adams

Body Goo 1 Sneezing

Body Goo 2 Burping

Body Goo 3 Farting

Body Goo 4 Vomiting

Body Goo 5 The Crusty Bits

Body Goo 6 The Sticky Bits

Love Bugs Don't Step on The Ant

Love Bugs Don't Splat The Spiders

Printed in Great
Britain
by Amazon